Life of a Stickman

(The New Neighbor)

Season 1

On June 4th 2013, Stickman Jr. woke up early in the morning due to fighting noise he heard from his back yard that had broken his sleep. Stickman Jr. got up out of his bed to see what and who was making noise and he saw that it was his new neighbor that lived upstairs apartment that was practicing karate in his ninja suit. After Stickman Jr. finish peeking and spying on the new neighbor whose name was Sticky, he went back to his room and fell asleep.

Five minutes later Stickman Jr. was disturbed again by noise coming from the backyard. So Stickman Jr. got out of his bed again and went outside in the backyard and saw that the new neighbor that was in a ninja suit was now shooting hoops on its noisy backboard. So Stickman Jr. asked the new neighbor Sticky wasn't it too early for basketball, and then the former ninja turned and smiled and Stickman Jr. saw how crazy he looked and he got scared and then he went back to his room. Stickman Jr. lied in his bed until he fell asleep again.

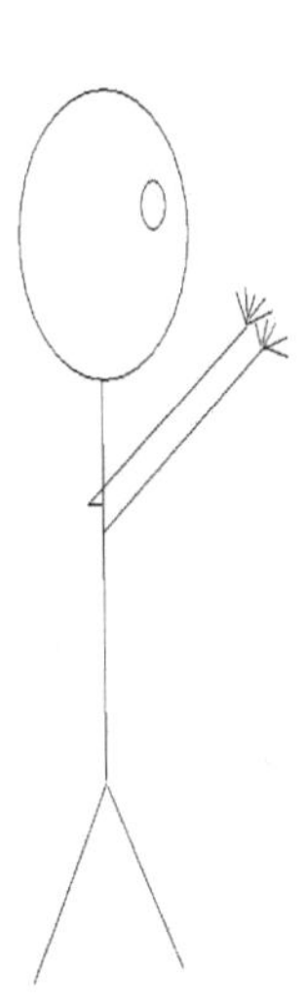

After ten minutes this time, Stickman Jr. was disturbed again; this time by dog barks. So he got out of bed once again and went in the backyard and saw the dog. Stickman Jr. asked the new neighbor Sticky if he can keep it quiet and Sticky agreed and stopped playing with his dog.

So Stickman Jr. went back in his
room to lie back down. Before he
can go to sleep, his dad (Stick Sr.)

Came in his room and told him
that he was leaving for work and
Stickman Jr. said okay. After
Stickman Jr. found the silence he
was looking for, he drifted away to

sleep. But suddenly he was disturbed again so he went out in the backyard and saw that Sticky was skating around doing tricks with his skateboard. So Stickman Jr. asked sticky "didn't I told you to keep it quiet", he said. And the new neighbor told him that he thought he was talking about the dog. So Stickman Jr. got upset and went back in the house to his room.

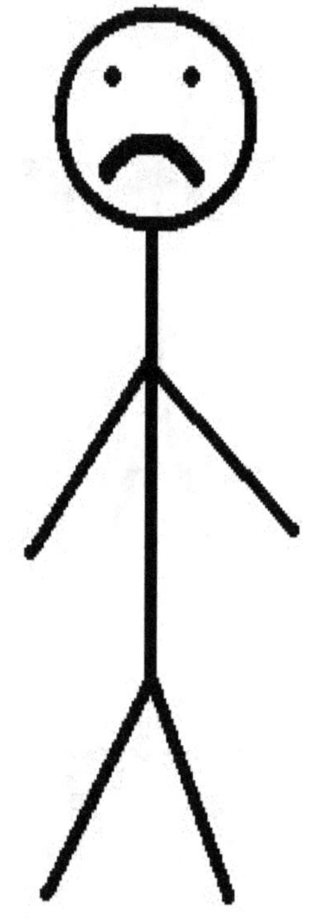

So this time Stickman Jr. didn't go
back to sleep, he just waited for
the next annoying noise from his
new neighbor. After not hearing
any noise, Stickman Jr.
surprisingly got out of his bed and
went to see what Sticky was doing
but he didn't see him in the
backyard so he gladly went back
in his room and jumped on his bed
and fell asleep as fast as he can.
But unfortunately, Stickman Jr.
woke up again due to the strong
smell of paint. So Stickman Jr. got
up to see who was painting, and

soon he got outside, he witness Sticky painting the side of the house. Stickman Jr. asked him why was he painting and sticky the neighbor said that it was his routine and told Stickman Jr. that he couldn't wait for tomorrow to do it all over again. Stickman Jr. asked him what did he mean do it all over again and Sticky told him that he couldn't wait to practice karate, play basketball, play with his dog, skate and paint. Stickman Jr. asked him do he do that stuff every day and Sticky told him that he been doing it for 10 years straight. Stickman Jr. didn't respond, he just went back in the

house and started thinking. And
finally he came up with an Idea.

After it was dark outside and sticky
went inside and fell asleep,
Stickman Jr. saw the opportunity
to ruin his next day so he went
and erased Sticky's ninja sword,
his basketball, his dog, his
skateboard and his paint.
Stickman Jr. was so happy he
erased all of Sticky's things so that
he can finally have some peace.

The next morning, Sticky woke up
as early as possible and then he
went in the closet to find his ninja
suit and then he put it on. Next, he
went outside to practice his karate
but he was confuse because he
didn't see his sword where he left
it. He was major upset but he got
over it and went to get his
basketball. He was searching for
his basketball for hours until he
gave up. Sticky was very upset
that he couldn't find his ball. Next
he went to his dog house and
called out his dog's name
(Angelica) but he didn't hear no
noise so he looked in his dog
house and saw that it was empty.

After he finish crying because he couldn't find his dog, he went to get his skateboard so that he can do some tricks but he was dumbfounded when he couldn't find that neither. Next, he went to find his paint so he could finish painting but he couldn't find that too.

Meanwhile Stickman Jr. was having a lovely dream, but his dream came to an end when he heard loud knocks on the door. Stickman Jr. got up to see who it was, and he saw that it was his new neighbor that was asking him to play with him. Stickman Jr. told him it was too early to play, so he closed the door and went back to sleep. In the next hour, Stickman Jr. was broken out of his sleep again by knocks on his door, and when he opened it, Sticky asked him to play with him because he was bored. So every hour, he knocked on the door and asked Stickman Jr. to play with him until he gave in and finally said yeah.

For two months straight, Stickman Jr. played with Sticky routinely until he finally got an Idea of how to get away from him. When Stickman Jr. had time to himself, he erased his body except for his hands and walked on his hands until it bumped into something and then he drew his body back. He saw that he was a couple of blocks away from Sticky and was very satisfied. Sticky was upset that he couldn't find his friend (Stickman Jr.) so he drew up a StickFinder (GPS) and typed in "stickman JR." in the search field until the "StickFinder (GPS) showed where was Stickman Jr. located.

Stickman Jr. was having a celebration in his new house until the bell rang and he ran towards hoping that it was his father but to his surprise; as soon as he opened the door, Sticky rushed and gave him a big hug. Stickman Jr. couldn't do nothing but cry and then he grabbed the eraser.

Life of a Stickman

(The Wrong Home)

On June 8th Stickman Jr. purchased a piece of land on Madison Avenue to build a house, street number 581.There were no houses on that street because a tornado came through and tore everything down in May. So while that street was empty, Stickman Jr. decided to rebuild a strong house made out of bricks so that a tornado would have a hard time blowing it down.

Two days later on June 10th, Stickman Jr. began to work on his project. He went to the brick store to purchase 500 bricks to build his new house. It took him 5 hours to transport all the bricks from the store to his new purchased property. Once he finish transporting all of the bricks, he realize that it was too dark to work on his house so he left all of the bricks there until the next day. So he went back to his dad's house (Stickman Sr.) to stay there for a couple of nights until he finish his house.

Stickman Sr. was a 70 year old Vet who liked to talk war stories. Every day he drowned his son Stickman Jr. with stories that took

hours to finish. Stickman Jr. tries
to avoid his dad so he can avoid
those long stories because they
became annoying most of the
time.

When Stickman Jr. walked in, his
dad smiled and told him that he
never got to finish that story last
night and Stickman Jr. said it was
okay, but Stickman Sr. insisted
that he finish the story because he
thought it was rude that he fell
asleep while telling him the story
last night.

So his dad continued the story and said: *The boat exploded and six of us was in the middle of the ocean, so we took off our back packs and our guns and watched them sink in the sea, so that we can have less weight on ourselves, and then we swam for five hours until we got to shore. Luckily we did a lot of training in earlier days to be able to complete this difficult task. But when we finally got to the shore, our enemies had pointed guns at us and we were weaponless because we tossed our armory in the ocean. So what happen next was that we were taking as P.O.W*

Right after Stickman Sr. said that, he fell asleep again but Stickman Jr. was happy that he did so he can go to his room and go to sleep himself.

The next day Stickman Jr. woke up early in the morning and was happy that it was nice and sunny outside so that he can work on his house. Another reason he was happy so that he can get out of the house away from his dad.

Once he got to his new street, he saw bricks on other land next to his, so he went to work and started building his house with bricks. After doing a lot of hammering and pasting, he finally took a break after working for 3 hours straight. When Stickman Jr. got his rest he went back to work but then it started to rain so he left his tools and ran home to his dad's house. When he approached his dad's house, he saw that his dad was talking to two little girls who were selling him candy and he was talking to them about his days in the war, so Stickman Jr. snuck around the

back and entered the house from
the back door.

The next day Stickman Jr. went
out to work on his house and he
was almost done with it. About
after four hours, he finally finished
his house of bricks and was very
happy about it. He was so happy
he took out his camera and began
taking pictures. Then an old
person came up to him and
thanked him for the house.
Stickman Jr. became curious and
then asked the old fellow why he

was thanking him, and the old fellow pointed towards his land and told him that he built his house for him. Stickman Jr. looked at him crazy and told him that he purchased the 581 property and then the old fellow picked up the street number that was on the ground and the piece of line that goes to the 7 number and showed him and said this property is 587. Sweat started to pour from stickman Jr. face and then he cried while walking back home to his dad's house because he was very upset that he did all that work for nothing.

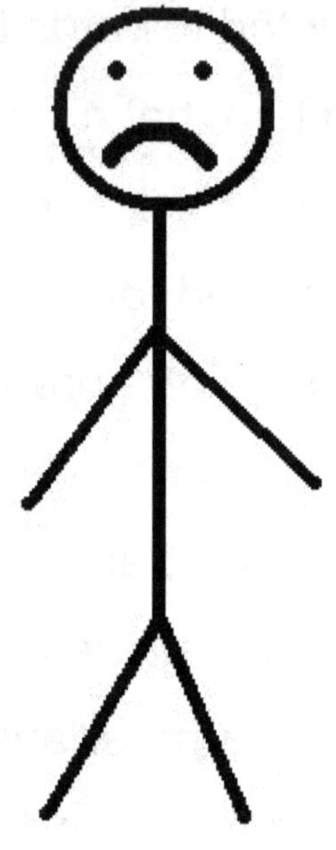

Life of a Stickman

(Sometimes the gender and name don't match)

On August 1st it was a rainy day so Stickman Jr. went to the library to find himself a book to read. He went to the young adult section and took out a book called "The Caged Bird That Wouldn't Sing". He sat down and opened the book but before he could read his first word, his eyes caught the most beautiful stick walking towards the romantic book section. From then on his eyes were glued to this beautiful stick. He closed his book he was about to read and went up to the romantic book section of the library. He pretended to pick a book next to the beautiful stick and blindly picked out a book called

"Hunted By Love" and he looked at her and smiled. She commented that was a good book and Stickman Jr. told her that it was one of his favorites. Then she asked him what was his favorite part and he started laughing and then he switched the subject and asked her for her name. She said her name was Stickerah in a soft beautiful voice. Stickman Jr. told her it was a pretty name and then he introduced himself. Next, he asked her what book was she reading and Stickerah grabbed the "Love Poems" and told him that she was borrowing this today. Stickman Jr. lied and told her that

he writes poems and then she
asked him could she read it and
he told her that he was bringing it
tomorrow. So they left the library
and went home.

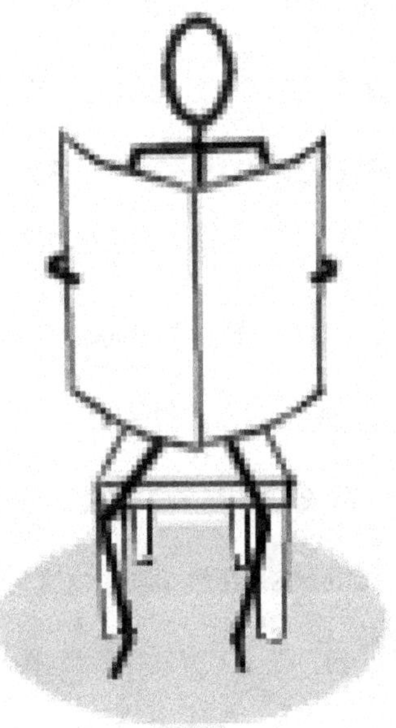

Stickman Jr. was still staying with his dad until he find a new home. Stickman Jr. started pacing back and forth because he realized that he don't know how to write poetry and felt like he was in a predicament. Then he got a paper and pencil and wrote one line that said "Roses are red, violets are blue" and then he gave up because he couldn't think of any more words. Then his dad stickman Sr. came in and he was so happy to see his son. He put his groceries on the kitchen table and then came and sat next to stickman Jr. and asked him where did he left off at. Stickman Jr.

shrugged his shoulders and said he didn't know. Then stickman Sr. said "Oh yeah, now I remember" and then he went on to continue his war story.

Once we made it to land after hours of swimming, guns were the first thing our eyes saw so we surrendered and our enemies took us as P.O.W. We traveled through a wild life jungle because they were taking us back to their main base to put us in jail. It was painful as I can remember because we were all warn out and they still made us walk through the jungle.

Sadly one of our men fainted and died because he was too tired to go on. I cried silently like a fish because I didn't want our enemy to smell fear. Then suddenly, "cough cough; hold on son, cough cough".

Stickman Jr. ran to his dad when he started coughing and asked him was he okay. His dad struggled to speak so stickman Jr. told him not to say anything and told him to rest so he can finish the story at another time. His dad agreed with his son and then he went to sleep. After Stickman Jr.

saw his dad sleep, he picked up
his paper and pencil and tried to
think of words to put on the paper.
After hours passed, Stickman Jr.
fell asleep with his paper on his
lap and his pencil in his hand.

The next morning Stickman Jr.
went to the library hoping that
Stickerah forget about the poem.
When he got there, she was
already sitting down reading a
book. Stickman Jr. sat down next
to her and said what's up.
Stickerah responded by saying the
sky is up, jokily. They both
laughed and Stickman Jr. went on

and told her that he liked her.
Stickerah replied and told him that
he was a nice stick and then she
asked him for the poem. Stickman
Jr. was sweating nervously
knowing that he messed up, so he
told her that he didn't finish
because he was taking care of his
dad. She asked him about the
other poems that he written and
then Stickman Jr. told her that he
lost the poems. Stickerah giggled
and asked him was he really a
poet. Stickman Jr. looked down
and said no as he felt like he was
a liar. Stickerah got up and
announced "since you finally told
the truth, I must tell the truth too"

she said. Stickman Jr. face got curious and asked her what was she talking about. Stickerah looked away fearing to make eye contact and then she told him that sometimes a name and gender don't match. Stickman Jr. was still lost so he said that he was clueless of what she was saying. Stickerah took off her wig and socks out of her shirt and told Stickman Jr. that she's really a man. Stickman Jr. froze from those exact words and the he collapse and fainted.

HUH?

The Life of a Stickman

(Stickman Jr. Gets a Job)

On August 21st Stickman Jr. was woken up by his dad. His dad yelled at him and told him to cut the grass. Every two weeks Stickman Jr. dad makes him cut the grass in the front yard. One day Stickman Jr. said he was tired of cutting grass for his dad so he went and got the morning paper and searched for a job in the jobs section. When Stickman Jr. saw a job that he liked, he called the job number and asked them if they are hiring. The speaker on the other end was talking in a different language from Stickman Jr. which he couldn't understand; so he hung up the phone. So Stickman

Jr. waited for the next day to go
look for a job.

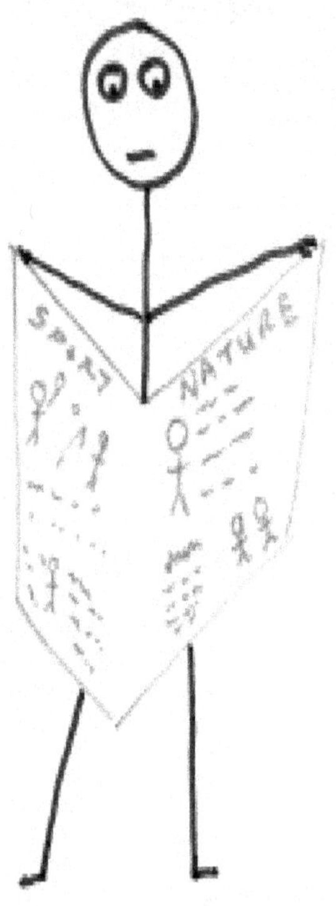

SPIRIT
NATURE

After Stickman Jr. fixed his bed so he can lay down, his dad came in and told him that he missed a spot on the front yard. So Stickman Jr. went back outside to cut the grass again until it looked perfect. When he was done, he went in his room and got back in his bed. But before he can go to sleep, his dad interrupted him again and told him that he was just trying to make him a responsible young stick. And then he went on to continue the story that he never got to finish because he was coughing too much.

Instead of burying one our men, our enemies just left him there for the wild animals to feast on. I only cried inside because I didn't want to show our enemy any fear so I refused to shed a tear. Meanwhile we made it to the P.O.W camp where they kept all of their opposing soldiers like us for ransom. But before they put me in one of those crusty looking cages, they took me to this room where 3 big enemies staring down at me with their evil eyes, installing fear inside me, so I looked away to avoid it. Their boss came up to me and asked me where was my army base located, and I just kept silence. So the boss got mad and slapped me. That slapped was so hard it almost put me to sleep. So they interrogated me for two more hours until they realize that I was loyal to my army. So the next thing was one of the enemies came toward me with a needle and I can't remember what happen next, all I know that my mind went black.

Stickman Jr. started snoring very loud so that his dad can stop speaking. Stickman Sr. realize that his son was sleep so he stopped telling the story and went out the room. When he heard the door closed, Stickman Jr. peeked with one eye to see if his dad left and then he turned on the lamp and began staring at the newspaper to find a job that he liked.

The next morning, Stickman Jr. left the house early for job searching. At the end of that whole day he went to 50 stores to get a job but no one hired him because he was short and a young adult (19). So the next day Stickman Jr. wore sneakers that made him look 2 feet taller and then he went to the same stores that he went to yesterday and spoke in a heavier voice to make him sound older. Still no one hired him because they all said that he looked weird. Stickman Jr. grew tired of the discrimination so he started putting everything in the experience box including the things he didn't like; like cutting grass and washing cars. In the job experience box, he usually just put "Sales person" and "Driver" but this time he put everything to increase his chances of getting a job.

After two weeks passed, Stickman Jr. finally got a call for a job. The caller offered him a job and asked him to come by the next day to start. Stickman Jr. was so happy he got a job but he didn't even know what job he would be doing but he was excited anyway. The caller asked him to meet him at the tool store to pick up some tools for the job. Stickman Jr. said sure and hung the phone up.

The next day Stickman Jr. got up on time and ran to the tool store and he saw his dad there and asked him what was he doing here

and his dad told him that he was
buying a new lawn mower
because the old one broke. Then
his dad asked him what he was
doing here and Stickman Jr. told
him that he was meeting
somebody for a job. Stickman Jr.
got tired of waiting so he called the
number from the caller who called
him yesterday for a job; and then
his dad's phone rang and he said
hello. They both looked at each
other surprisingly as they notice
that they were talking to each
other. Stickman Jr. got worried
and asked his dad was it him that
called to hire and his dad said
"yeah I guess"

When they got home, Stickman Sr. gave him the lawn Mower and told him to get to work. Stickman Jr. whispered "I should never said I was a grass cutter on that stupid application".

Life of a Stickman

(A good day for Dad's story)

On September 7th it was a rainy
day. Stickman Jr. watched the
weather channel and saw that it
was going to rain all day so he
sighed because he didn't want to
stay in the house all day. He was
so bored that he didn't know what
to do and then he got up and tried
to do some exercise but he got
tired and lost motivation quick
because of the look of the rain.
The rain made him feel lazy and
sleepy the way it made music on
the windows. Stickman Jr. took out
some board games but his dad
wasn't there so he had to play by
himself. The first board game he
played was checkers and he

pretended that he was playing his dad. After he jumped all his men, he cheered that he was the greatest checker player in the world. Then he played monopoly but he quit early because he found it too complicated to play by himself. He got tired of the board games, so he took out the twister map and started playing twister.

He realize that it was no fun playing by himself so he thought of another game. "Oh, connect 4", he said. So he played connect 4 and made the black chip win all the games. He used his left hand as an opponent and his right hand as himself. He enjoyed it for a while but realize that he was cheating for his right hand when he was making bad moves with his left hand all the time. Finally Stickman Jr. got sick of the board games, so he played hide n seek with the brooms and the mops. But he realize that the brooms and the mops wasn't looking for him so he quit. Then he sat back on the couch and turned the TV on. This time the TV wasn't working because the rain was interfering with the satellite dish that they had. So Stickman Jr. cried because he was suffering from boredom.

Then his dad came in and
Stickman Jr. jumped up for joy
because he was happy to see him.
His dad asked him was he okay
and Stickman Jr. told him that he
was bored. His dad told him that
he was going to go lay down and
Stickman Jr. yelled "Noooo" , "tell
me a story before you go to sleep
", he said. Then his dad asked him
where did he left off at from the
war story and Stickman Jr. told
him that the boat exploded
somewhere. Then his dad said
"Oh yeah" and so he continued his
story and said:

The boat exploded and six of us was in the middle of the ocean so we took off our back packs and our guns and watched them sink in the sea, so that we can have less weight on ourselves so we don't drown. Then we swam for five hours until we got to the shore. Luckily we did a lot of training to be able to swim that long. But when we finally got to the shore, our enemies pointed guns at us and we surrendered because we didn't have any weapons because we left it in the bottom of the sea. They chained us and we became P.O.W and they made us travel through a wild life jungle because they were taking us to their P.O.W camp to interrogate us and throw us in cages. It was painful as I can remember because we were all warn out and they still made us walk through the jungle. Sadly one of our men fainted and died because he was too tired to go on. I cried silently like a fish because I didn't want our enemy to smell or see fear. I was upset that they left him there instead of burying him. Finally we got to the P.O.W camp where they kept all of their enemies for ransom. But before they tossed me in those spikey crusty dirty cage, they took me to a room where three huge guys staring me down installing fear in me, so I looked away to hide it. Then their boss came to me and asked me where was my army base located. I just kept silence and then the boss got mad and slapped me. That slapped was so hard it almost put me to sleep. So they interrogated me for two more hours until they realize that I was not telling them anything they wanted to hear. So the boss gave one of his soldiers the signal and then he came towards me and stuck a needle in me. "Wait wait son, I forgot the rest of how that story goes, I'll be right back"

Stickman Jr. dad went to his room and after 5 minutes he came back with a book that said "Days in the army". And then he opened it up and continue to read, but Stickman Jr. stopped him and asked him where did he get the book? And his dad told him that he got it from the library, that this was a best seller. Stickman Jr. got confused and asked him who story was this and then his dad told him that it's just a fictional story by Jerry Ayers. Then Stickman Jr. stood up and said "Wait a minute, so this wasn't a story about you?

And his dad replied and said no son and told him that he was a Veterinarian not a Veteran. Stickman Jr. told him that he thought he was in the army all this time and then he ran and jumped out the window.

Project Dreams

In this story, two twins (Rasheed and Shareef) have dreams of making it out of the hopeless ghetto but many obstacles get in their way that make their dreams further away.

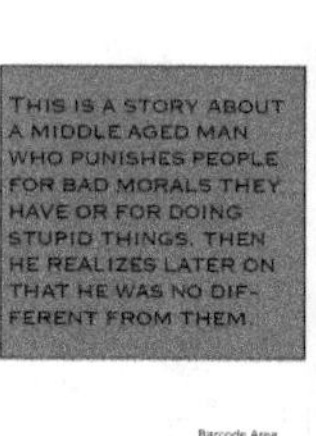

The Punisher

This is a story about a middle age
man who punishes people for bad
morals they have or for doing
ungodly things, then he realizes later
that he was no different from them
and set out to punish people
differently.

Adopted for Hope

This is a story about a mother who prostitutes herself and her young daughter and then when she gets arrested, one of her new customers takes her daughter in.

The Slave

Similar to "Roots" but this story is a fantasy of what many wish that happened instead. The whites thought that they was profiting off of a slave but later they found out that they captured the wrong slave, the slave that hunted each and every one of them. Horror

Horror Stories

READ AT YOUR OWN RISK

High School Massacre

A young boy who been bullied in school grows up to be a cop and seek revenge on the ones that bullied him.

Love Poems

Poems about love

School Trip

Teacher's rewards a class of students gets rewarded to go on a special school trip on the last day of school, but they were surprised when they reached their destination. Comedy. Very Funny. A bus ride full of fun.

Caged Bird That Wouldn't Sing

A very touching story that discovers the reality of the justice system...A Caged bird that wouldn't sing is a metaphor and a poetic story that searches for justice within the jail cell. In this story, not all birds belong in the caged.

Hunted by Love

Falling in love is a healthy feeling but it isn't safe, especially not in this story. Not only the cheater says the wrong name when doing it, they may say the wrong name when dreaming...This is a mind twister with a little bit of love, horror, intense, drama and everything else. There's a lot of truth to it, especially when you dreaming or drinking because all the truths comes out.

The Sleep Over

A story about someone who seeks revenge at a family sleepover which was supposed to be a get together party for the family but instead it turned into a terrifying nightmare especially for the younger ones. A story about someone who seeks revenge at a family sleepover that was supposed to be a get together party for the family but it turned into a terrifying nightmare especially for the young ones. A happy family get together party turned into a horror episode once night fell.

Another Rose

If you read the poem then the story is a must read. A story truly inspired by the greatest Tupac. A best seller and book of the year. This is a book inspired by the late great Tupac Shakur...One of the most interested story you can possibly read. If you read the poem (the rose that grew from concrete) then you need to read the story...This story extends from the original poem by Tupac Shakur (The Rose That Grew From Concrete) to give people a good insight of a

rose that really grew from concrete
and how it faces obstacles in life
because it was looked at as
abnormal. Inspired by Tupac Shakur

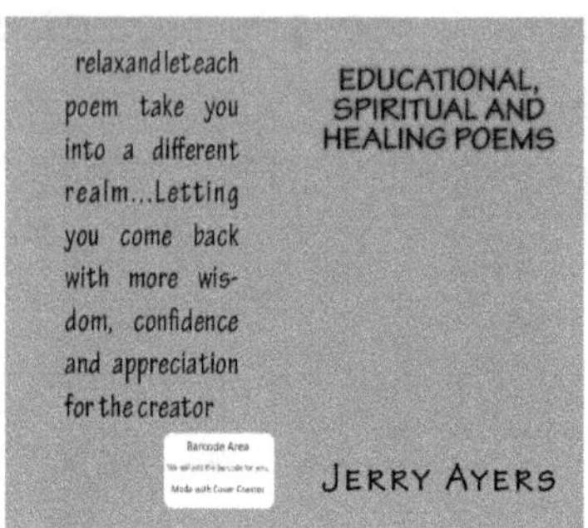

Educational, Spiritual and Healing Poems

Relax and let each poem take you into a different world. You're guaranteed to come back with more wisdom, confidence and appreciation.

16 and Pregnant

If you are 16 and thinking about getting pregnant or have a child that's 16 and pregnant then this book is perfect for you. Very educational for young girls who sees pregnancy as glory at a young age but they learn everything about true experiences of being pregnant. Read the life a young 16 year old who had a baby at 16 and thought her life would change for the better but it changed for the worst. Educational

Bullied

About a young kid being bullied in school. He goes through so much in such a little time. This book is meant to raise bully awareness across the world. This is one of the best bully awareness book in the world. In this terrifying life this kid goes through, he faces bullies, teachers, himself, his parents and his suicidal thoughts.

Love Me More

Jaliah son, Jahsir finds a way to express his love for his mother; but in a way he thought that she would love him more...his mother was left with confusion from the beginning to the end but when she finds out, she's even more shocked. A Mother and Son love story.

Like Sister Like Brother

A mind twisting story about a sister and brother always fighting but something made them realize that they were all that they needed. Once they figured out what they thought they didn't have and realize what they wanted, they gave each other the best thing they can ever give- brotherly and sisterly love.

The Unlucky Summer

This is a story about 2 cousins who been annoyed by their older cousins who came and took over, so they try to make plans to get rid of them, like the kid in home alone (similar story) only learning that they made a bigger mistake and wish they can take everything back...

Funniest Jokes

Treat yourself with the world's funniest jokes

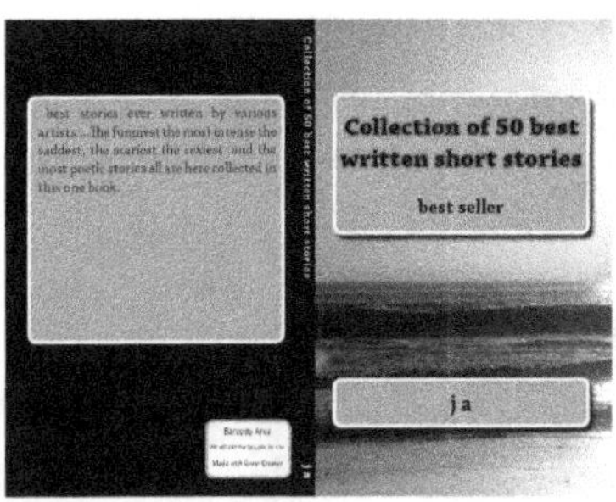

Collection of 50 best Short Stories

The world's best short stories ever written. Written by various famous writers across the world. The funniest, the scariest, the most intense, the most educated and the most poetic stories are all here put together in a collection in this book. You can take this book of stories everywhere you go and show it off. Over one million sold in book stores worldwide. Now it's finally available on Amazon so don't miss out.

Roses

A young lady guided by roses to help her find her lost daughter

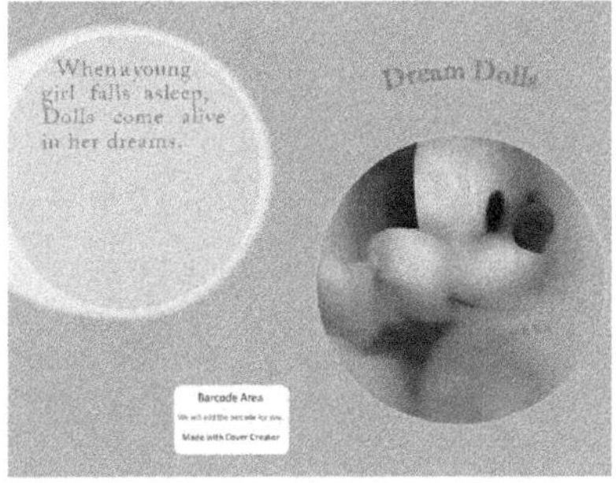

Dream Dolls

When a little girl falls asleep, dolls come alive in her dreams

Life of a Stickman

A Stickman goes on a journey of different experiences

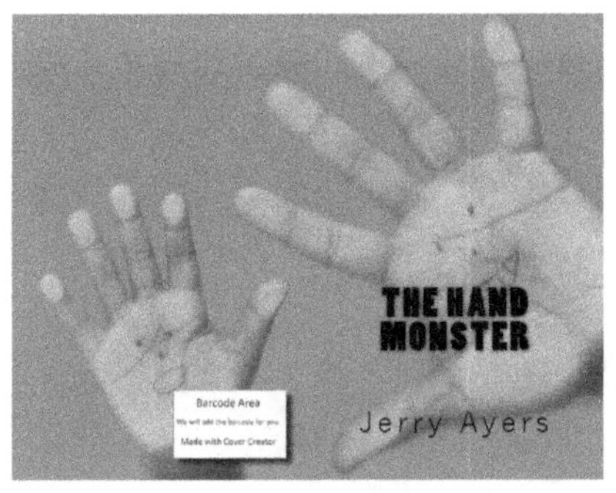

The Hand Monster

A horror story for children

A 9 year old
girl dreams of
growing up to be a
professional cheer-
leader.

Cheerleader

Cheerleader

A 9 year old girl dreams of growing up to be a professional cheerleader

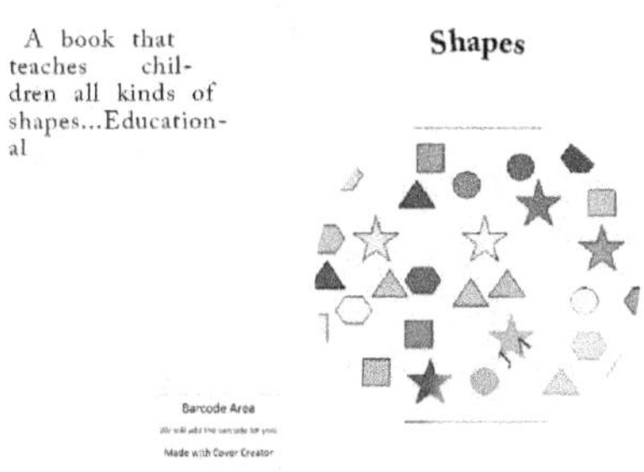

Shapes

A list of all the shapes so children can learn

Barbie World

5 little girls finds a hole in a mysterious tree that has a hidden portal which leads to a new world, Barbie World.

Undivided We Fall

Chanel was a pregnant prostitute who sold her body to support her drug addiction, who twin daughters were separated at birth due to a tragic event that took place. Her daughter's grew up not knowing either one of them existed. They both went through their own struggle in life that brought them together as one...... by Gerald Toatley projectdreamsbooks.com is a website created by innovative writers that focus on educating the minds with very well written Urban, Children, Poetry, Educational and even Adult Books to influence in a positive way and providing high-quality service and customer satisfaction - we will do everything we can to meet your expectations.

With a variety of books to choose from, we're sure you'll be happy working with us. Look around our website and if you have any comments or questions, please feel free to contact us.

We hope to see you again! Check back later for new updates to our website. There's much more to come!

This is a website that sells books to raise money to help support Charities such as Feeding The Children, Children's Hospitals, Diabetes Campaign, Bully Awareness Programs, Cancer Patients, Homelessness and many other Charities. So basically each book you buy, you will be giving money back to one of these charities. All books are positive and fun to read that has a great influence on the readers. You can choose a category from " YOUNG ADULT AND CHILREN'S BOOKS", OR "URBAN BOOKS", OR" POETRY BOOKS", OR "EDUCATIONAL BOOKS" AND EVEN POSITIVE "ADULT BOOKS". So there's many different types of books to choose from that which you may like. If you want to help support this website "projectdreamsbooks.com succeed in raising money for charity, you can spread the message to as many people or friends you know and you can also donate money by contacting us and sending us information of how much you want to donate.

Thank You for your support

Projectdreamsbooks.com